P9-DDT-105

Disney's
A
Christmas
Carol

Adapted by James Ponti

Based on the classic story by Charles Dickens

Based on the screenplay by Robert Zemeckis

Produced by Steve Starkey, Robert Zemeckis, Jack Rapke

Directed by Robert Zemeckis

Disney PRESS
New York

Printed in the United States of America
First edition
1 3 5 7 9 10 6 8 4 2

Library of Congress Catalog Card Number on file.
ISBN 978-1-4231-1790-2

Prologue

Jacob Marley was dead.

That much is certain. There will be points during this story when a reader might wonder if in fact he was still alive or perhaps if it was merely a rumor that he had died. But rest assured that Jacob Marley took his last living breath in London on Christmas Eve 1836.

His lifeless body was laid to rest in a plain wooden coffin in a dank woodworking shop behind a mortuary. There were no flowers to brighten the mood, no somber organ music to mark the occasion, no friends or family sobbing at the loss of the dearly departed. The only ones in attendance were a dour undertaker, his young apprentice, and Marley's longtime business partner, Ebenezer Scrooge.

It is worth noting that in this very cold and dark room, on a snowy winter's day, there was nothing as cold and dark as the heart that beat inside Ebenezer Scrooge. As he looked down at the corpse of the man who had been his partner for as long as anyone could remember, there was no emotion or sense of loss.

If anything, Scrooge seemed annoyed at the necessity of having to come down to identify the body and serve as a witness at the funeral.

Marley's bony hands were folded just above his waist, his thinning hair had been pulled back, and his tiny spectacles rested on his pale, colorless forehead. He looked as if he might be asleep—except for two very notable exceptions. The first was the bandage that ran under his chin and was tied at the top of his head. This was not because of any wound or injury. It was to keep Marley's face from contorting in death. The second was the fact that, as was the custom, a copper penny had been placed on each of Marley's cold, dead eyes.

"Yes," Scrooge said with no hint of sadness in his voice. "Quite dead. As a doornail."

Scrooge looked out the open door and saw a team of black horses hitched to a gleaming black hearse. Steam continuously flowed from their nostrils into the cold December air. They would carry Marley's body to its final resting place.

Scrooge could scarcely entertain the thought that Marley might still impact his life from the grave. In fact, all he was thinking about was the waste of money this extravagance represented. To his figuring, a simple wagon with a single horse could have done the job for less money.

Although Scrooge had no warmth in his heart for his dead partner, or for any living person for that matter, there was one thing he loved: money. His entire life had been dedicated to earning and holding on to as much money as possible. He was very good at it and had become a wealthy man.

He also begrudged every penny that left his greedy fingers. That explained why Jacob Marley's funeral was taking place in a woodworking shop surrounded by half-finished cabinets and barrels rather than in a funeral home.

There was no minister with a sermon, and Scrooge was not about to give a eulogy, so the only official duty that needed to be attended to was the signing of the death certificate. The undertaker handed the document to Scrooge, who examined it carefully before scrawling his wretched signature across the line marked *Executor*.

When he handed the document back to the undertaker, Ebenezer had an uneasy look about his face. Something was upsetting him. This emotion, however, had nothing to do with the passing of Jacob Marley and everything to do with the passing of money from him to the undertaker. His craggy fingers reached into his purse and painfully pulled out three coins to pay the man.

Oh, what a tightfisted, squeezing, wrenching, grasping, scraping, clutching, covetous old sinner this Scrooge was! Hard and sharp as flint, from which no steel had ever struck a spark of warmth. This cold within him froze his features, nipped his pointed nose, shriveled his cheeks and made his eyes red and his lips blue.

Those thin, blue lips were closed as tight as his purse as he handed the money to the undertaker. They remained that way until the young apprentice started to close the lid on the coffin.

"Stop! You fool!" Scrooge barked.

Both the undertaker and his apprentice stepped back. They thought that maybe this horrid man was finally ready to show an appropriate emotion. They wondered if he wanted to take one last look at his friend. Maybe he wanted to whisper some earthly farewell.

Scrooge sneered at them in disgust, reached over and plucked the copper pennies off the dead man's eyes.

The two men watching him gasped, but Scrooge cared not one bit. He slipped the money into his purse and turned his cold red eyes toward theirs.

"*Tuppence,*" he said, using the English term for two pennies, "is tuppence!"

Scrooge did not even give his dead partner a final look! He just turned and went out into the snowy afternoon.

As Scrooge walked back to his office, he was surrounded by the sights and sounds of the holiday. Green garlands and Christmas wreaths hung in every doorway. Last-minute shoppers and street vendors crowded the narrow cobblestoned streets. Children and carolers assaulted his pointy ears with their joyous laughter and singing.

It was almost more than he could bear.

He saw two young boys secretly grab hold of the back of a passing carriage. It pulled them along the icy bricks as if they were on skates. They were as happy as could be at their little game, but Scrooge just shook his head in disgust.

"Delinquents!" he muttered as he continued his trek along Whitechapel High Street.

If Scrooge hadn't been in such a hurry to get back to his office and earn some more money, he might have noticed an amazing occurrence. Despite the fact that Whitechapel was the poorest section of London, the people were surprisingly happy. They didn't have much, but the spirit of Christmas had moved them to celebrate what was good in their lives.

Although Scrooge undoubtedly had more money than any of the people he pushed by that Christmas Eve, he was also the least happy.

It is no coincidence that the word *miser*, which is used to describe someone who is stingy with his money, also contains the first five letters of the word *miserable*. Both of these words described Ebenezer Scrooge.

But what did he care? He liked to edge his way along the crowded paths of life, his cold, heartless eyes warning everybody to keep their distance. It would take much more than the spirit of Christmas joy to warm the heart of Ebenezer Scrooge.

And, for the next seven years, no one even tried.

Chapter 1

It was seven years to the day since Jacob Marley had died, and Ebenezer Scrooge had not changed one bit. He still only cared about money, and he still detested the happy people walking up and down the streets wishing one another a Merry Christmas. Not even the weathered sign outside his office had changed. Despite the fact that his partner had long been in the grave, it continued to read: SCROOGE AND MARLEY.

He hadn't kept both names on the sign as some sort of tribute to or remembrance of Marley. He simply refused to spend the money it would have cost to have a new sign made.

Scrooge and Marley was a countinghouse, a business that traded and loaned money. Scrooge's fortune was earned through the troubles of others. In moments of emergency or great need, businesses and people came to him to borrow money. He loaned it under the condition that in addition to repaying the loan, they also paid an exorbitant fee.

Times were hard, which meant that business was good. Scrooge's company was very successful. But none of those profits had been used to improve the looks and conditions of the bleak and dreary offices.

On this Christmas Eve, Ebenezer was hunched over the desk in his darkened room as he carefully counted the coins from an iron strongbox, a thick metal box that he used to hold and protect his money. While he did, he made notations in a ledger book that tracked each and every penny that passed through the company.

He always kept his office door open so that he could keep a watchful eye on his one employee, a clerk named Bob Cratchit.

Cratchit was the opposite of his boss in almost every way. While the old man was rich and kept his riches for himself, the clerk used his meager salary to support his loving wife and children. His mood was also very different from Scrooge's. He was kind and friendly and usually had a bright smile on his round face.

This Christmas Eve, however, his teeth were too busy chattering to smile. The countinghouse was so cold that the ink in his inkwell had frozen solid. In order to make a mark on his ledger, Cratchit had to hold the tip of his quill pen over a candle to warm it enough to melt a spot of ink.

There was a heating stove by Cratchit's desk, but it offered no warmth. Scrooge only allowed him to burn a single lump of coal at a time. It scarcely provided the slightest bit of heat.

Cratchit looked at it and saw that it was barely glowing.

Cratchit desperately wanted to pull a few more pieces from the coal box inside Scrooge's office, but he knew that it was pointless to even wish for such things. Ebenezer kept the box locked and hung the key from his belt. If Cratchit wanted any warmth, the best he could do was to rub his hands over the small candle on his desk.

When a sudden gust of wind caused the flame to flicker, Cratchit turned to see the door swing open. It was Scrooge's nephew, Fred, whose cheerful voice boomed a greeting as he closed the door behind him. "A merry Christmas, Uncle! God save you!"

At first glance, it was hard to imagine that Fred and Scrooge were related in any way. The young man was tall and handsome with a ruddy complexion, his face red from having walked through the cold.

Despite the lively entrance, Ebenezer barely

looked up from his desk. "Bah, humbug!" he spat out as he continued his counting.

"Christmas a humbug?" Fred laughed. "Uncle, you don't mean that!"

Scrooge momentarily stopped his counting and looked up at his nephew. "Merry Christmas," he muttered. "What reason have you to be merry? You're poor enough."

Fred shook his head in disbelief. "What right have you to be so dismal?" he retorted. "You're rich enough!"

Scrooge didn't know what to say to this, so he resorted to his favorite term. "Humbug!"

Fred was determined to cheer his uncle. "Don't be cross," he said as he walked over to his desk.

Scrooge would have none of it. "What else can I be when I live in such a world of fools as this?" he asked. "Merry Christmas? What's Christmastime to you but a time for paying bills without money? A time for finding yourself a year older and not a penny richer?!"

To emphasize his point, Ebenezer waved a ruler at his nephew. "If I could work my will," he said, his voice filling with anger, "every idiot who goes about with 'Merry Christmas' on his lips should be boiled in his own pudding and buried with a stake of holly through his heart."

"Uncle!" Fred cried. Even for Scrooge this was mean-spirited.

"Keep Christmas in your own way," the old man continued. "And let me keep it in mine."

"But you don't keep it."

"Let me leave it alone then," Scrooge replied. "Much good it has ever done you."

Fred grabbed hold of his lapels as if he were giving an important speech. "There are many things from which I have derived good and have not profited. Christmas being among them," he proclaimed. "But I've always thought of Christmas as a kind, charitable time when men open their shut-up hearts and think of all people as fellow travelers to the grave and not some other race of creatures bound on other journeys. Therefore, Uncle, though it has never put a scrap of gold or silver in my pockets, I believe it has done me good, and I say, God bless it!"

Bob Cratchit was so impressed with Fred's little speech that he couldn't help but burst into applause.

Scrooge spun around and waved his ruler at Cratchit. "Let me hear another sound out of you," he warned the clerk, "and you'll keep Christmas by losing your situation."

Cratchit tried to look innocent. He quickly stumbled off his stool and poked at the lone lump of coal in his stove.

Scrooge snickered and turned back to Fred. "You're quite a powerful speaker," he taunted. "It's a wonder you don't go into Parliament."

"Don't be angry, Uncle," Fred begged him. "Come, dine with us tomorrow."

Scrooge narrowed his eyes and stared hard at the young man. "I'll see you in hell first."

Cratchit couldn't believe what he was hearing. Neither could Fred. But rather than anger he only felt sorrow for his uncle.

"Why so coldhearted?" he asked.

"Good afternoon," Scrooge said, dismissing him.

"I want nothing from you," Fred said, unwilling to budge. "I ask nothing of you. Why can't we be friends?"

"Good afternoon," Scrooge said, turning back to his work.

Fred merely shook his head. "I'm sorry with all my heart to find you so resolute," he said. "But I have made the trial in homage to Christmas. Therefore, a merry Christmas, Uncle! And a happy New Year!"

"Good afternoon!" Scrooge said for the final time.

On his way out the door, Fred stopped by

Cratchit's desk and shook the clerk's hand.

"A very merry Christmas to you, Mr. Cratchit."

"And merry Christmas to you, sir," Cratchit replied with a hearty smile.

Upon hearing this, Scrooge stopped counting and looked up at his employee. "There's another one," he said, scowling. "A clerk making fifteen shillings a week, and with a wife and family, talking about a merry Christmas."

The smile quickly disappeared from Cratchit's face and he went to latch the door behind Fred. Before he could, two portly men came in carrying books and papers.

"Good afternoon," one of them said as he checked a list he was carrying. "Scrooge and Marley's, I believe?"

Cratchit pointed toward Scrooge's office. They took off their hats and presented Scrooge with credentials that showed that they worked for charity.

"Have I the pleasure of addressing Mr.

Scrooge or Mr. Marley?" asked one of the men.

Scrooge hardly looked up from his work. "Mr. Marley has been dead these seven years," he said with a scowl. "He died seven years ago this very night."

The man nodded solemnly. "We have no doubt his generosity is well represented by his surviving partner," the man replied.

"At this festive season of the year, it is more than usually desirable that we should make some slight provision for the poor and destitute. Many thousands are in want of common comforts," he said, hoping that Scrooge would donate to their good charity.

He had no idea what kind of man he was dealing with.

Scrooge narrowed his unforgiving eyes. "Are there no prisons?" he asked.

The men weren't sure what he meant by that. "Plenty of prisons," one replied.

"And the union workhouses," Scrooge

continued, referring to the dreadful institutions where those who were too poor to support themselves were forced to live. "Are they still in operation?"

"They are," the other man answered. "I wish I could say they were not."

"Good!" Scrooge said, feeling that prisons and institutions were all the poor deserved. "I was afraid something had occurred to stop them in their useful course."

The two men exchanged a worried look.

"At this festive season," one responded, "a few of us are endeavoring to raise a fund to buy the poor some meat and drink and means of warmth. What can we put you down for?"

"Nothing!" Scrooge spat. "I can't afford to make idle people merry! I support the establishments I have mentioned, and those who are badly off must go there."

"Many can't go there," the other man tried to reason. "And many would rather die."

This brought a smile to Scrooge's face. "Then they had better do it," he told them. "And decrease the surplus population! Good afternoon, gentlemen!"

The two men exchanged horrified looks and quickly left the countinghouse. There were no more disturbances for the remaining hours, and not a word was spoken until it was time to close up shop.

"You'll want all day tomorrow, I suppose," Scrooge sneered, angered at the mere idea of having to give the clerk a day off for Christmas.

Cratchit gulped. "If quite convenient, sir."

Scrooge shook his head. "It's not convenient, and it's not fair," he replied.

"It's only once a year, sir," Cratchit said hopefully.

"A poor excuse for picking a man's pocket every twenty-fifth of December," Scrooge said as he put away his ledger book and pulled on his coat. "But I suppose you must have the whole day. Be here earlier the next morning."

Cratchit quietly put out his candle, arranged his desk, and headed for the door. He watched as Scrooge carefully triple-locked the door and turned to walk home. Only when the old man had started up the street one way did Cratchit run off in the opposite direction.

In a matter of seconds, the clerk weaved through the crowds of people like a happy child excited about the holiday. Around the corner he came across a group of children taking turns sliding down an icy hill.

"In honor of Christmas Eve," he announced as he joined them. He tried to slide down the hill carefully, but quickly picked up speed, lost his balance, and fell on his bottom. The children erupted in cheers and laughter.

Scrooge, meanwhile, found his way to a dark and lonely tavern for dinner. The only other customer was a drunken man who had passed out on a table, still clutching a cup of ale.

Ebenezer was eating a revolting bowl of kidney stew. When he raised a spoonful of the foul brown mush to his lips, he gagged at the smell. He had to force himself to put it into his mouth and once he had gulped it down, he dropped his spoon.

"Waiter," he called out. "Waiter!"

A sweaty, red-nosed waiter came over to him. He was wearing a filthy apron covered in dried blood and grease.

"There's something wrong with this stew," Scrooge protested.

The waiter wiped his hands on his apron and looked down at the disgusting mush. "Fresh yesterday," he said. He reached over, grabbed a crock of mustard, and slapped it down on the table in front of Scrooge.

"Bah!" Scrooge barked as he dumped a giant dollop of the mustard into the stew in a vain attempt to mask its horrible taste.

After forcing down his repulsive dinner,

Ebenezer walked toward his house on Lime Street. Unlike the road to Cratchit's home, there were no children running around, excited about Christmas. There was just Scrooge, his lonely steps echoing off the empty cobblestones. A lone streetlight cast an eerie glow in the thick London fog.

Scrooge saw a mangy rat scurry across the sidewalk in front of him. With lightning speed, Ebenezer pinned the rat's tail with the heel of his boot. The old man cackled with joy as he tormented the little rodent, poking at it with his walking stick.

Suddenly the rat turned and let loose an evil hiss that startled Scrooge. He fell back a step and the creature darted away into the darkness.

"Take that, you filthy vermin," Scrooge snapped as he took a feeble swing at the rat with his stick.

Many years ago, Scrooge's house had been grand and beautiful. But over time it had become rundown and gloomy. The once luxurious parlors and rooms were now just dark and eerie. It was the type of house children avoided walking near because it seemed haunted.

The rusty gate squeaked when Scrooge pushed it open and shuffled up the brick path toward his front door. The fog had now grown so thick that the outlines of the house were not clearly visible. It appeared to be nothing more than an inky shadow at the top of the street.

As he approached the front door, Scrooge fumbled with his key and dropped it. It clinked against the stone entryway and Ebenezer had to bend over and search for it.

While he was bent over, he could not see that a pale, dismal glow had begun to surround the large bronze knocker on his door. It continued to get brighter, and when Scrooge finally located his key and stood up, the knocker had transformed itself into the shape of Jacob Marley's face.

Scrooge let out a scream and jumped

back. He stared in horror at the ghostly image of his late partner. Marley's eyes were shut, and his hair floated in every direction.

Scrooge stared for a long moment, wondering if his eyes and the fog were playing tricks on him. The only way to be certain was to reach out and touch the knocker.

He extended a trembling finger to the knocker's ring, which appeared to be clamped in Marley's mouth like a horse's bridle. Just as he was about to grab hold of the ring, Marley's eyes popped open!

There was an earth-shattering crack as the knocker came to life. The eyes looked right into Scrooge's, and the mouth flew open.

Scrooge spun backward and fell off the stoop, slamming down hard onto his tailbone.

"Owww!!!!" Scrooge yelled, turning to run. But as he took one last frightened look at the knocker, it appeared to be normal. There was no terrifying face or eyes, just an old bronze knocker that had been there since the house was first built.

Scrooge shook his head, angry at himself for letting the fog play tricks on him. He took a deep breath and quickly unlocked the door. As he opened it, he took a moment to peek around the other side, to see if by some supernatural twist, Marley's pigtail was hanging out of the back. He was relieved to find that there were only screws and nuts holding the knocker in place.

"Pooh, pooh," Scrooge muttered to himself.

It was pitch black in the entryway until Ebenezer struck a match and lit his candle. The flickering light cast eerie shadows throughout the cavernous room as he slowly began to climb the stairs. Each step made a loud creaking noise.

Behind him, the shadows began to change shape and reform themselves into a terrifying image. As if he could sense what was happening, Scrooge spun around in time to see the cloudy images come together as a foggy version of the hearse that had carried Marley to his grave. Pulling the hearse was a team of monstrous black stallions charging right up the stairs after him.

The sound was deafening, and Scrooge pressed his body against the wall just as the phantom team streaked past him and vanished into thin air.

Scrooge did not know what to make of any of this. Shaking in fear, he took a deep breath and aimed his candle at the front door, making sure that it was still bolted shut and chained.

"Bah!" Ebenezer said, once again angry at himself for letting his mind play such tricks on him.

That night as he dressed for bed, he was in an even fouler mood than usual. The droning on about Christmas, the visit from his nephew, Fred, and now these ghostly reminders of Jacob Marley had his head in a twist.

He sat next to the small fireplace in his bedroom and stirred a pot of gruel, hoping that the terrifying visions had come to an end.

He looked around to see that everything was in its proper place. The drapes of his four-poster bed were pulled open just as they were supposed to be. The sofa and table stood silently in the same arrangement in which he had left them. The fire-poker, the washbasin—everything was just as it always was.

Satisfied that everything was right, Scrooge settled down into his chair and began to eat his gruel.

He only swallowed one spoonful before the flame in the fireplace came to life and started to spark and sizzle. Scrooge nervously pulled his legs up close to him. He looked at the flickering light as it illuminated the tiles surrounding the fireplace.

These tiles had pictures of Cain and Abel, pharaohs and angels, and all sorts of images from the Bible. Scrooge was momentarily relieved to see that things were as they were supposed to be.

But then the images on the tiles began to change, reshaping themselves into images of Jacob Marley.

Terrified, Scrooge looked directly at the fireplace. Right before his eyes, the smoke and fire transformed into the same ghastly image of Marley that had been at the front door. Only now, a flame flickered through the spirit's mouth like a fiery tongue.

Ebenezer rubbed his eyes for a moment and when he looked back at the fireplace, the flames were normal and the pictures on the tiles looked the same as they always had.

"Humbug!" Scrooge said with an angry snap of his head.

He got up and walked to his bedroom door, checking the lock to make sure that both bolts were slammed shut.

He slowly went back to his chair by the fire and sat down. He looked back at the door and noticed a dusty old bell that once had been used to signal from room to room.

Without the slightest breeze, the tiny bell began to swing back and forth, but it made no noise. Then slowly, it began to sound a faint *ding-a-ling*, which grew louder and louder until it became a thunderous clanging that forced Scrooge to cover his ears.

When it finally stopped, everything was silent for a moment before Scrooge heard a *plink*. He looked over to the source of the sound and saw that a penny had fallen from his jacket pocket. He realized that it wasn't just any penny. It was one of the copper pennies that he had taken from Marley's dead eyes. Moments later, there was another *plink* as the second penny fell from his pocket.

Scrooge trembled in fear as these two pennies rolled away, making little circles on the floor before disappearing under the door and out into the hall.

Scrooge was now fully terrified. He heard the bone-chilling sound of the front door creaking open. It was the same door that he had locked three separate ways.

He did not know where to turn or what to do as he listened to the loud, clanking sound of someone dragging heavy chains up the stairs echo through the house.

Scrooge stopped breathing and wished that all of this would come to an instant and merciful end.

It didn't.

Once they reached the top of the steps, the footsteps could be heard walking down the hall to Scrooge's bedchamber.

Ebenezer was white as the sheet on his bed and too petrified to move when the footsteps stopped on just the other side of his door.

Suddenly, a loud crashing could be heard as four huge, ghostly strongboxes came flying through the door and landed on the floor. The strongboxes were somewhat transparent and otherworldly. They were chained to something on the other side of the still-intact door.

Scrooge shook uncontrollably, his knees knocking beneath his nightgown. His eyes were focused on the door where another wrenching sound signaled that something else was passing through.

A glowing, ghostly substance began to form on the inside of the door. And, though he knew in his heart what this was, he pleaded to himself that it not be so. The substance began to form itself into the shape of a giant phantom that stood seven feet tall.

Just then the flame in the fireplace came back to life and formed a pair of eyes and a mouth. The flame screamed the words that Scrooge could not let pass through his own lips: "It's Marley's ghost!"

Chapter 2

Although he could see through the terrifying specter floating right in front of him, Scrooge was certain it was Marley. Marley's face looked the same as it had in the coffin seven years earlier, with the bandage wrapped the long way around his face. A lengthy phantom chain was tied around his waist, and attached to it were the huge cashboxes, keys, padlocks, ledgers, and other objects that had seemed so important to him in life.

Much like Scrooge, Jacob Marley had cared little for anything other than money when he was among the living. Now, all the objects associated with earning money were his permanent burden.

"How now," Scrooge called to him. "What do you want with me?"

"Much," the giant ghost said, drawing the single word out into a long guttural call that echoed through the room.

Scrooge tried to mask his fear and demanded, "Who are you?"

The ghost was facing him, but his eyes were wild and unfocused. "Ask me who I was," he instructed.

"Who were you then?" Scrooge asked, sounding a bit angry when he did.

The apparition floated a little closer, and Scrooge tried not to tremble. "In life, I was your partner, Jacob Marley."

"Can you sit down?" Scrooge asked.

"I can," the ghost answered.

Scrooge didn't believe him. He could see right through the specter's body to the buttons on the back of his coat.

"Do it then," Scrooge ordered.

Marley shrunk down to nearly normal size and lowered himself into a chair on the opposite side of the fireplace. As he did, his phantom chains clanged loudly.

It unnerved Scrooge that he could see right through this being. Even though the ghost was sitting, Ebenezer could still clearly see the chair he was sitting in.

"You don't believe in me," the ghost said, his hair and clothes floating as if they were being blown by some phantom wind or were in some deep, unseen water.

"I don't," Scrooge insisted

"Why do you doubt your senses?"

"Because the littlest thing can affect them," Scrooge explained. "A slight disorder of the stomach can make them cheat. You may be an undigested bit of beet, a blot of mustard, a crumb of cheese, a fragment of underdone potato."

He adjusted himself in his seat and stared right at the ghost. "There's more of gravy than of grave about you. Whatever you are."

Marley's ghost suddenly started growing and growing until he was giant once again. As he grew, he rattled his chains and let out a frightful cry. "Aaaaahhhhh!"

Scrooge's bravado immediately vanished. He realizaed that he was in the presence of his former partner, and there was no place he could run or hide. Terrified, Scrooge fell to his knees and pleaded. "Dreadful apparition, why do you trouble me?"

The creature looked down at him. "Man of worldly mind, do you believe in me or not?"

"I do!" Scrooge replied, nodding and trembling at the same time. "But why do spirits walk the earth? And why do they come to me?"

The spirit wafted in the air, floating back and forth ever so slightly. "It is required of every man that the spirit within him should walk among his fellow men and travel far and wide.

Marley stared directly into Scrooge's eyes. "And if that spirit goes forth not in life, it is condemned to do so after death! It is doomed to wander through the world and witness what it might have shared on earth and turned to happiness!"

Because he had not cared about his fellow man in life, he was forced to do so after death. Just saying the words made Marley's misery that much worse, and he let loose a terrifying wail that rattled his chains.

"You are fettered in chains," Scrooge said. "Why?"

Marley's ghost shook his head mournfully. "I wear the chain I forged in life. I made it link by link, yard by yard. Do you recognize the pattern?"

The ghost held up a length of chain for Scrooge to examine. Trembling, Ebenezer looked at it and shook his head no. He quickly realized the chain was the physical representation of human greed. Marley's chains were great in number because of the selfish way he lived his life.

"Can you imagine the weight and length of the chain you bear?" Marley questioned. "It was as heavy and long as this seven Christmas Eves ago. Yours is a ponderous chain."

Scrooge turned and scanned the floor, almost expecting to suddenly find a ghostly chain connected to him. Although he was scared of Marley's ghost, he realized an even greater fear was growing inside him, the fear of what might await him in death.

"Jacob," he implored the spirit, "tell me more. Speak comfort to me!"

Marley's wild eyes focused and burned into Scrooge's. "I have none to give," he intoned as he slowly began to float away in the air. "I cannot stay. I cannot linger anywhere. Mark me! In life, my spirit never walked beyond our countinghouse. Never roved beyond the narrow limits of our money-changing hole! Now endless journeys lie before me!"

Scrooge reached toward him and pleaded. "Seven years dead and traveling the whole time?!"

"The whole time! No rest, no peace!" Marley replied. "I was blind! Blind and could not see! My whole life squandered and misused! Oh, woe is me!"

Scrooge was confused. Nothing about Marley's life seem misused to him. "But you were always a good man of business."

"Businesssss!" Marley bellowed so violently that the bandage snapped, causing his entire jaw to fall off.

Scrooge reeled back from the horrible sight of Marley's chin dangling from a ghostly string of bone, making his mouth a gaping, hideous hole. When Marley tried to talk again, he could not form words until he used his hand to move the chin and mouth up and down.

"Mankind was my business," he continued, his rotted teeth clicking as they gnashed together. "Common welfare was my business! Charity, mercy, forbearance, and benevolence were all my business!"

Scrooge cowered in fear as Marley retied the bandage around his head.

"Hear me!" he implored Scrooge. "My time is nearly gone."

Scrooge trembled and shook as he pleaded. "I will. But don't be hard upon me, Jacob!"

Marley gave Scrooge a deathly serious stare that penetrated deep into the old man's soul.

"I am here to warn you, that you yet have a chance of escaping my fate," he explained. "A chance of my procuring, Ebenezer!"

"You were always a good friend to me, Jacob," Scrooge replied gratefully.

"You will be haunted by three spirits," said Marley's ghost.

"That's my chance and hope?" a frightened Scrooge replied. "I'd rather not . . ."

The ghost interrupted him with a blood-curdling cry. "Without their visits, you cannot hope to shun the path I tread," he roared.

Scrooge watched in horror as the ghost flipped its chains around his arms and floated backward toward the window. As he did, the window slowly began to open with a spine-chilling creak.

"Expect the first tomorrow when the bell tolls one," Marley said.

Scrooge was terrified of what awaited him. "Couldn't I take them all at once and have it over with, Jacob?"

As Marley floated past Scrooge, he looped one of his chains around the bottom of the frightened man's chair, slowly turning it toward the opening window.

"Expect the second one the next night at the same hour and the third upon the next night, when the last stroke of twelve has ceased to vibrate."

The window was now completely open and the room was filled with the echo of painful wails, the sounds of the regret of spirits who spent their lives pursuing the wrong goals.

Marley floated out the window and levitated in the air outside Scrooge's house. Suddenly, he yanked on the chain so violently that it pulled Scrooge over to the window, slamming his bony legs against the sill.

"Look to see me no more," the ghost said as he floated into the cold, dark night.

Pinned against the wall by a chair, Scrooge looked out through the window and gasped. The sky was filled with thousands of moaning, sobbing phantoms! They were spirits like Marley, forever wandering aimlessly in restless haste to make up for lives ill-spent.

Every one of them was burdened with heavy chains. Some were even chained together, partners in crime forced to spend eternity with their shared shame.

One in particular caught Scrooge's attention. It was the ghost of an old man who had a monstrous iron safe chained to his ankle. The man cried in agony as he looked at a still-living woman and baby begging on the street. The two were extremely poor and in desperate need of money. The man had obviously ignored such people when he was alive, but now he wailed at his inability to help them from the grave. His greed had sentenced him to this eternity, and Scrooge could not help but see that his own life had been little different.

Quickly, the street and sky filled with more spirits like these, millions of condemned souls shrieking in agony. Their cries rattled Scrooge, and he clamped his hands over his ears in a desperate attempt to block out the dreadful noise.

Suddenly, a horrible, half-rotted phantom

flew right toward him, screaming all the way. Scrooge lunged backward and toppled out of his chair, crashing down onto the floor.

He scurried across the room and dived into his bed, pulling the blanket up over his head, wishing that he might suddenly awake and learn it had all only been a dream.

Chapter 3

Scrooge cowered beneath his blanket until he lapsed into a cold and fearful sleep. When he finally snapped awake, he had no sense of the time or of how long he'd been asleep. His ferretlike eyes darted back and forth, and he was too frightened to open the curtains that surrounded his bed.

"Was it a dream?" he whispered to himself.

The silence was broken by a riotous clang coming from a nearby church bell. If this sound was supposed to be at all musical, it was not. For Scrooge it was terrifying. He prayed silently, hoping the bell would strike at least one more time, but it did not. That meant it was one o'clock, the time Marley had informed him that the first spirit would arrive.

Scrooge pulled the covers up to his chin and pressed his bony body back against the headboard of his bed as he braced himself for what might happen.

Suddenly, his bed curtains flew open and a blinding light flooded the room. Scrooge held his hands up in front of his face, shielding his eyes from the light. After a few moments, his eyes adjusted enough for him to see.

He was face to face with a shaft of hot white light. The beam was large and focused and came from below his bed. It swept across the room as if somehow there were a giant lighthouse hidden below him.

Scrooge rattled in fear. He wanted to disappear and avoid all of this. But Marley said that Scrooge needed to face these spirits if he wanted any hope of avoiding a miserable existence in which he dragged the chains of his life for all eternity. After a long moment, he summoned enough courage to peek over the edge of the mattress, and there he saw another ghostly apparition.

Unlike Marley's ghost, this spirit did not remind Scrooge of anyone he had known. He had the shape of a child but the features of a very old man. He had long, silvery white hair but not a single wrinkle or age spot on his face. The specter wore a pure white tunic tied with a shimmering belt.

The strangest and most unnerving thing about the creature to Ebenezer was the pulsing light that sat upon his head like the flame that flickered atop a candle. Under his arm he carried a large gold cap that looked as if it were designed to put out candles.

"Are you the spirit whose coming was foretold to me?" Scrooge asked.

"I am," the ghost said as a sprig of holly

magically appeared in his hand.

"Who and what are you?" Scrooge asked.

"I am the Ghost of Christmas Past," he answered.

"Long past?"

"Your past," the ghost said as he reached for Scrooge and took him strong by the arm.

"Rise," the ghost said. "Walk with me!"

Scrooge, still in his slippers, nightgown, and nightcap, suddenly started floating in the air above the bed. The ghost tilted his head and shone his beam on the far wall. The light started to flicker, blinking faster and faster, like a movie projector, until images began to appear.

Scrooge and the ghost floated through the window, but when they got outside they were not hovering above Lime Street late at night. They were in an altogether different time and place, flying through a land that seemed to be projected from the light atop the spirit.

"Good heaven!" Scrooge said as he looked

down over the snow-covered country road. "I was bred in this place. I was a boy here."

The spirit gently touched Scrooge's arm. "Your lip is trembling," he said. "And what is that upon your cheek?"

Scrooge quickly wiped away a tear. "Nothing," he muttered, embarrassed at his show of emotion. "Something in my eye."

"Do you remember the way?" the specter asked.

Scrooge couldn't help but smile. "Remember? I could walk it blindfolded."

Scrooge and the spirit continued to float over the quiet road until they came to rest in the center of the town.

Scrooge was startled by the noise of three boys riding toward them on horseback. He went to get out of the way, but the ghost gave him a reassuring pat on the arm.

"These are but shadows of the things that have been," said the ghost. "They have no consciousness of us."

The boys raced right past Scrooge, completely unaware of him. Soon another group of boys appeared riding in a country wagon driven by a farmer. These boys shouted and sang as they waved handmade banners announcing GOING HOME and MERRY CHRISTMAS.

"*Here we come a wassailing,*" they sang joyously as they rode past.

"I know them," Ebenezer said, his eyes brightening at the memory. "I know every one of them. They were schoolmates of mine."

"Let's go on," the ghost said with a kindly smile. The images from his light continued to project until they arrived at an old, redbrick schoolhouse.

"This was my school," Scrooge said with a sniffle.

"This school is not quite deserted. A solitary child, neglected by his friends, is left here," said the ghost.

Scrooge had to fight the urge to cry. "I know."

Scrooge and the spirit floated through the walls and along the empty halls of the old building until they came to a long, narrow classroom.

Alone in the classroom was young Ebenezer Scrooge, only seven years old. As he looked out the window at the falling snow, the young Scrooge sang in an angelic voice:

Adeste, fideles—
Laeti triumphantes—
Venite, venite in Bethlehem—

As he watched himself as a young boy, he thought back to another young boy he had snapped at, and tears began to well up in Scrooge's eyes. "Poor boy," he said, wiping the tears with the cuff of his nightgown. "It's too late now."

"What's the matter?" asked the spirit.

"Nothing," Scrooge said. "There was a

boy singing a Christmas carol at my door last night. I should have liked to have given him something."

The spirit nodded. "Let us see another room." With a wave of his hand the classroom began to crumble in front of them. The wood from the walls splintered, the windows cracked, and chunks of plaster fell from the ceiling. When the dust settled, they were in the same room, only ten years later.

The young Scrooge faded into the darkness, and in his place a different Ebenezer Scrooge stepped forward. This Scrooge was seventeen years old. Despite his youth, he still had the same distinctive nose and neck of the old man. He walked through the school desks with a downcast look about him.

Suddenly, a little girl rushed into the room, threw her arms around the teenage Scrooge, and gave him a big kiss. It was Ebenezer's sister, Fan, only six years old at the time.

"Dear brother," Fan called out. "I've come to bring you home."

"Home?" the boy said, trying not to get too excited.

"Yes, home," she replied. "Father is so much kinder than he used to be. He spoke so gently to me one night. I was not afraid to ask him if you might come home. And he said yes!"

Young Scrooge looked down and smiled at his sister.

"He sent me in a coach to bring you," Fan continued. "We're to be together all the Christmas long. And have the merriest time in all the world."

The teenager knelt down and touched the cheek of his sister. "You are quite a woman," he said with a smile.

Little Fan stood on her tiptoes and gave her brother a hug.

The old Scrooge watched from above, touched by the memory. "She had a soft heart," he said quietly.

The ghost nodded, and the two of them started to drift backward, away from the children.

"She died a woman," the ghost said. "And had children."

"One child," Scrooge said with a nod.

"True," replied the spirit. "Your nephew."

"Yes," Scrooge said, suddenly feeling guilty about the way he had treated his nephew, Fred, when the young man came to visit him at his countinghouse.

While Scrooge considered this, the ghost changed direction, and with his flickering beam took Scrooge away from the countryside of his youth and to London.

They flew over a busy thoroughfare crowded with carts, coaches, and pedestrians. Everything was decorated for Christmas, and the two of them came to a stop outside a warehouse. Shafts of warm amber light came through the windows from within. There was a name painted above the door, and the sight of it brought a smile to Scrooge's face.

It said *Fezziwig*.

"Do you know this place?" asked the Ghost of Christmas Past.

"Know it?" Scrooge answered, his jaw dropping. "I was an apprentice here."

The image in front of them shifted, and they instantly found themselves inside the warehouse. There they saw a jolly old man sitting at a ridiculously tall desk.

"Why it's old Fezziwig," Scrooge shouted with glee. "Bless his heart. It's Fezziwig, alive again!"

The clock on the wall struck seven. Fezziwig put down his pen and called out, "Yo-ho, there. Ebenezer! Dick!"

Two young men dashed into the room. One was Ebenezer Scrooge, when he was twenty-seven years old. Unlike his future self, this Scrooge was filled with happiness and wore a big smile. The other was his fellow apprentice, Dick Wilkins.

"There he is," the older Scrooge shouted at the vision of his old friend. He turned to the Ghost of Christmas Past and continued. "Dick Wilkins. He was very attached to me."

Scrooge watched and laughed as fat old Fezziwig leaped from his high desk, flipped over, and landed on the floor, tumbling into a perfect roll.

"Yo-ho, my boys," Fezziwig boomed. "No more work tonight! Christmas Eve! Clear away, my lads, and let's have lots of room here."

The younger Scrooge and his friend Wilkins pushed a table out of the way as Fezziwig started clapping and singing a song.

The ghost continued to project the image, and time quickly sped up. As it did, the warehouse was suddenly decorated like a giant ballroom. Christmas greens hung from the ceiling, a fire roared in the fireplace, and long tables were covered with food.

Dozens of young men and women dressed

in their holiday finest danced and twirled to the music being played by a fiddler perched high on Fezziwig's lofty desk. No one, however, danced with as much happiness and enthusiasm as Fezziwig and his wife. They were kind and generous people, and the Christmas spirit filled them with happiness and joy.

Finally, the fiddler came to the end of the song and stopped to catch his breath.

"Well done, well done," Fezziwig called as the room roared with applause.

Fezziwig was exhausted from his celebrating and downed a cup of punch in a single gulp. "And now, kind fiddler," he said as he caught his breath. "If you please, it's time for 'Sir Roger de Coverly.'"

Fezziwig's request was greeted with a cheer from the others, and the fiddler took one last deep breath and started playing the fast song.

Old Scrooge was looking back at it all when suddenly the ghost moved the scene so that they were now close to a young couple dancing. It was Ebenezer and a pretty young woman named Belle.

Just the sight of her brought sadness to old Scrooge's heart. He was once so in love with her that seeing her now dancing with his younger self was more than he could bear. He turned away.

Mercifully, the ghost used his cap to somewhat dim the light, and slowly the images in front of them faded away.

The spirit pointed at the people as they disappeared from view. "A small matter to make these silly folks so grateful."

"Small," Scrooge said, thinking that it was a very large matter.

The specter nodded and resumed making his point. "This celebration cost old Fezziwig but a few pounds of your mortal money."

Before Scrooge could disagree, the ghost cast another image out before him. They were now in a back room of the warehouse, which had been turned into a small apartment for Ebenezer and Wilkins.

"Mr. Fezziwig chooses to make us happy," the young Scrooge said as he lay awake on his cot. "This happiness he gives is as great as if it cost him a fortune."

"Here, here," Wilkins said in agreement.

At times when they relived these moments from his past, Scrooge almost forgot about the ghost. The memories and emotions were so strong that it was as if he were not watching himself as a young man, but as if he were actually a young man once more. And, this being one of those moments, he so wanted to talk to his old clerk, Wilkins. He wanted to reconnect. But then he looked and saw the spirit and realized that it was impossible.

"What's the matter?" asked the Ghost of Christmas Past.

"Nothing particular," Scrooge said as he

tried to clear the emotion from his throat.

"Something, I think."

"No," Scrooge replied, shaking his head. "I should like to be able to say a word or two to my clerk just now. That's all."

The spirit nodded. "My time grows short," he told Ebenezer.

And, in an instant, they had left Fezziwig's warehouse and were transported to the office of Scrooge and Marley. It was several years later, and Ebenezer was in his early thirties. His face didn't yet have the harsh and rigid lines that now defined it, but there was a greedy and restless motion to his eyes.

Through the glass partition of the office, he could see his partner, Jacob Marley. Marley was young and hard at work organizing heavy, iron lockboxes. For a moment, Scrooge was frozen by the knowledge that those same lockboxes would be chained to him for all eternity.

Then he heard crying and looked down to

Ebenezer Scrooge heads home, where he will be visited by a series of ghosts!

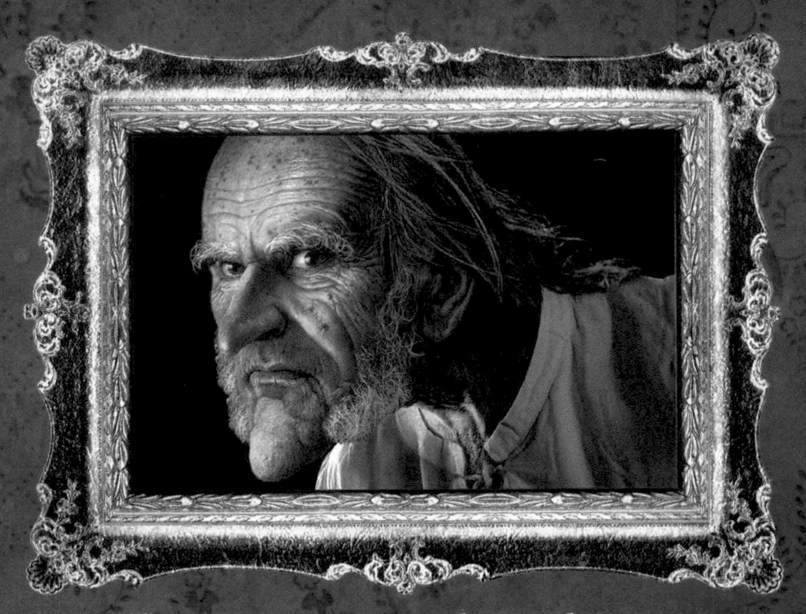

Scrooge is a mean and miserly man.

The ghost of Jacob Marley warns Scrooge of the spirits coming to his home.

The Ghost of Christmas Past shows Scrooge scenes from his youth.

Mr. Fezziwig's warehouse, where Scrooge had his first job.

The Ghost of Christmas Past introduces Scrooge to his younger self.

The jolly Ghost of Christmas Present
is next!

The Ghost of Christmas Present appears
with a mighty holiday feast!

The ominous Ghost of Christmas Yet to Come is the final spirit of the evening.

The Ghost of Christmas Yet to Come shows Scrooge the dark fate that awaits him if he doesn't change his ways.

Scrooge wakes up at home and realizes it is Christmas day!

Scrooge is thrilled to have another chance to live a good life.

Scrooge and Tiny Tim wish everyone
a merry Christmas!

see Belle, sitting next to his younger self. She was beautiful, but her face looked sad and tears lined her cheeks.

"Another idol has replaced me," she said.

"What idol?" the younger Scrooge asked.

Belle wiped the tears from her cheeks and stared him in the eyes. "A golden one."

Scrooge's success had changed him and now that he had earned money, he had begun to value it more than anything. Belle worried that he valued it even more than he valued her.

The younger Scrooge bit his lower lip and looked back at her. "There is nothing on this earth more terrifying to me than a life doomed to poverty," he told her. "May I ask why you condemn with such severity the honest pursuit of substance?"

Belle shook her head. "You fear the world too much, Ebenezer," she told him. "You've changed."

"Perhaps grown wiser," he explained to her.

"But I have not changed toward you."

"Our contract is an old one. It was made when we were both poor and content to be so," she said. "When it was made, you were another man."

The younger Scrooge was now getting angry. "I was a boy!"

Scrooge was heartbroken as he looked at his former self and the only woman he had ever loved. They had been engaged to marry, but it was at this moment that their engagement ended.

"I release you, Ebenezer," she told him.

"Have I ever sought release?" young Scrooge asked her.

"In words, no."

"In what then?"

"In everything that made my love of any worth in your sight," she explained. "Tell me, Ebenezer. If you were free today, would you choose a dowerless girl? A girl left penniless by the death of her parents. You, who weighs everything by gain?"

The young Scrooge said nothing. In his heart, he knew she was right. If he had his choice, he'd marry someone whose family had money and power. The older Scrooge could scarcely watch. Decades of lonely living had shown him that no monetary value could be placed on the love that he and Belle once shared. If only he had realized it at the time.

Belle wiped some more tears from her eyes and stood. She knew that she could never be happy with a man who only valued money. "I release you, Ebenezer," she said. "May you be happy in the life you have chosen."

As she walked from his office, tears streaked down the old man's face. "Spirit, show me no more," he pleaded with the Ghost of Christmas Past. "Conduct me home. Why do you delight in torturing me?"

"One more shadow," the spirit replied.

Just then, Belle opened the office door and a gust of wind blew in from outside. The gust caused the spirit's light to flicker, and with it many years passed.

When the flickering stopped, they were in a warm and pleasant house filled with noisy children. Everything about the room was bright and cheerful. Scrooge did not recognize it in the least.

Then he saw Belle.

She was older now and still radiantly beautiful. She sat by the fireplace talking to her teenage daughter. Ebenezer realized that the squealing children were hers. There were five in all.

"Father's home," shouted one of the boys.

Just then Scrooge turned to see Belle's husband enter the room. He was tall and handsome with a happy smile. He knelt down and hugged the children as they rushed over to him.

Just then, a porter walked in behind him, his

arms piled high with Christmas toys and gifts.

"Christmas presents!" the children shouted as they started to pull them from the porter's arms.

"All right, children," their father said, laughing and coming to the man's rescue. "These gifts are to reside in the foyer until Christmas. And no peeking!"

The children led the porter toward the foyer, and for a moment the noise died down.

"Where are we?" Scrooge asked the ghost. "And why do you bring me here?"

The spirit didn't answer; he just motioned for Scrooge to listen to Belle and her husband talk.

"I saw an old friend of yours today," the man said to her.

"Who was it?" asked Belle.

"Guess!"

"How can I?" she asked, and then a thought came to her and she flashed a smile. "Mr. Scrooge!"

Her husband laughed. "Mr. Scrooge it was," he told her. "I passed his office window and he had a candle inside."

For a moment Belle's husband stopped and his voice saddened. "His partner lies upon the point of death, I hear." He continued shaking his head. "And there he sat quite alone in the world."

Scrooge realized that this was the day that Marley had died. "Spirit," Scrooge said, turning to the ghost, "remove me from this place."

The spirit shook his head. "I told you these were shadows of things that have been," he reminded Ebenezer. "They are what they are. Do not blame me."

The swirl of emotion was overwhelming. "Remove me," he demanded. "I cannot bear it!"

Suddenly the ghost's face began to change into a quick succession of all the faces they had seen that night: young Scrooge, Fan, Wilkins, Fezziwig, and Belle.

Shaking with terror, Scrooge grabbed the golden extinguisher cap from the spirit and pressed it down hard on his head, covering the beam of light and finally putting out the flame.

"Leave me," Scrooge bellowed. "Take me back! Haunt me no longer!"

He pushed all the way down on the cap, and everything darkened until Scrooge was in a place that did not even seem a part of this Earth. It was a black void. But even still, some light seeped out from beneath the cap. This light pulsated faster and faster, brighter and brighter, until the golden cap began to vibrate and then erupt like a rocket thundering into the atmosphere.

Scrooge held on for dear life as they soared toward the heavens, the moon and stars growing larger and closer.

Ebenezer reached the end of his flight as he passed in front of the full moon. Then he began a terrifying drop back toward the Earth.

Falling like a rock, thousands of feet per second, he would have screamed but for the forces of motion and gravity that were pulling his face in every direction. When he punched through a cloud, he was able to see the Earth below. He hurtled toward England, then closer still toward London, and finally toward his house on Lime Street.

At breakneck speed Scrooge zoomed right toward the ridge that ran atop his roof. Just as he was about to slam into it, Ebenezer closed his eyes, too fearful to watch.

Somehow he passed through to his bedroom and slammed hard into the floor. After a moment of uncertainty, he caught his breath and realized where he was.

Unlike the visit from Marley's ghost, Scrooge had no doubt that what he'd just been through was real. And knowing that Marley had been right about the first ghost meant he was surely right about what was to come.

Scrooge began to rattle with fear as he looked toward the door of his bedchamber and saw a light suddenly pass beneath it.

Had the second spirit arrived . . . early?

Chapter 4

Scrooge struggled to avoid the light that was now streaming into his room from under the door. He jumped into his bed and attempted to pull the covers up over his head, but no matter how hard he tried, they wouldn't reach. Some unseen force kept stopping the blankets, tugging them away from his face and forcing him to look at the bloodred glow. The spirit had indeed arrived.

The bolt suddenly unlocked itself, and the door flew open. In an instant, the room was flooded with blinding light.

From inside the sitting room, a loud voice boomed, "Enter, Scroooooooge!"

Scrooge had absolutely no intention of getting out of his bed and going into the sitting room. But he didn't have much choice. To his horror, the bed was pulled by some unseen force and started to slide across the floor toward the door. When it got close, the bed jerked to a stop and flipped Scrooge up into the air.

He landed at the threshold of the sitting room, the blazing light almost blinding him. When he looked into the room, he could not believe his eyes. It was stretched completely out of its normal dimensions. The walls were forty feet tall and the ceiling looked like it belonged in a cathedral. Every inch of this gigantic room was decorated for Christmas. The walls were covered with fresh evergreens, holly, mistletoe, and ivy.

A roaring fire blazed in a massive fireplace. And piled in the middle of the floor as if on some sort of throne were heaps of holiday food: turkeys, geese, game hens, barrels of plum pudding, luscious pastries, and delicious steaming bowls of punch. Sitting on top of this mighty throne was a giant nearly fifteen feet tall wearing a green robe trimmed in white fur. The giant had dark brown curls that hung long and free alongside his kindly face. On top of his head sat a holly wreath draped with glistening icicles.

It was the Ghost of Christmas Present, sparkling, cheery, and joyful. He held a burning torch and lifted it to cast a light on Scrooge.

"Come in and know me better, man," the ghost instructed Scrooge.

Scrooge realized that there was no way to avoid this so he shuffled into the room, his head hanging low as he nervously looked down at his slippers.

"I am the Ghost of Christmas Present," the spirit bellowed. "Look upon me!"

Scrooge nervously looked up at him.

"You have never seen the likes of me before?" asked the ghost.

"Never," Scrooge answered, shaking his head.

The specter asked, "Have never walked forth with my elder brothers?"

"I don't think I have," Scrooge answered honestly. "You have many brothers?"

The ghost smiled. "More than eighteen hundred," he answered with a laugh. "Eighteen hundred forty-two, to be exact."

It took Scrooge a moment to realize that there was one brother for every Christmas. Then he noticed that the ghost had a belt with an ancient scabbard that had decayed and been eaten by rust. The scabbard was empty.

"I see you wear a scabbard but no sword," Scrooge said.

"Indeed," the ghost answered as he shot Scrooge a sharp look. "Peace on earth. Goodwill toward men."

"Spirit," Ebenezer said, resigned to the fact that there was no avoiding the lesson this ghost was about to teach him. "Conduct me where you will."

"Touch my robe," the spirit instructed him.

Scrooge reached toward the robe with his bony hand. When he touched it, the ghost started to shrink, collapsing its gargantuan frame down to a slightly more manageable nine feet.

He tipped his torch and out poured sparkling magic dust that twinkled on the floor. As the dust settled, the floor became transparent as if the boards had turned to glass.

The image startled Scrooge and he jumped back, worried that the glass might break. But it held firm just as though it were still wooden. Next, the ghost poured out some more of his magic dust, and the room suddenly started to rise straight up.

Terrified, Scrooge pulled himself closer to the ghost as the room detached from the house and started floating above the streets of London. Scrooge looked down on the world below him and saw a young boy in his Sunday clothes trudging through the snow and pulling a bright red sleigh.

"Very strange," Scrooge said nervously.

"Indeed," agreed the spirit. "Not many mortals are granted a heavenly perspective of man's world."

The two of them flew over London, and everywhere they looked, they saw people happily enjoying the spirit of Christmas, showing goodwill to one another. They passed through the dingy smoke coming from chimneys and brushed over the freshly fallen snow that blanketed the rooftops of the city. At one point, the ghost saw two men arguing, and he diverted their vehicle until it hovered over them. He sprinkled some magical dust from on high and when it landed on the two, they quickly went from fighting to laughing with each other as they walked arm in arm.

Next, the room flew over London to a part

of the city known as Camden Town. Here they swooped down over a small brick building, and the ghost poured out another helping of his magic dust.

"I take it this pauper's bleak dwelling is of some significance," Scrooge said.

The ghost gave Scrooge a wry smile and nodded toward the house. "'Tis all your loyal clerk can afford," said the spirit, "for his meager fifteen bob a week."

Scrooge sighed at the realization that this pathetic home was where his employee, Bob Cratchit, lived. The ghost lowered the flying room, and it magically passed through the roof of the house until they were looking down on the cramped home.

In the kitchen, Mrs. Cratchit and her fourteen-year-old daughter, Belinda, were preparing Christmas dinner. It was a warm and loving scene, and both were smiling and joking with each other. Suddenly two more of the

Cratchit children hurried in from outside.

"Mother," cried the young girl, "we just came by the baker's shop . . ."

Before she could say another word, her little brother finished the sentence. ". . . and smelled our goose. Cooking delicious."

Mrs. Cratchit looked at the clock above the fireplace. "Whatever got your precious father then?" she asked them. "And Martha? She wasn't as late last Christmas Day."

The little girl looked out the window and smiled. "Here she is," she announced. "Here's Martha."

Moments later, Martha, the eldest Cratchit daughter walked into the house carrying bags and packages. The younger children all surrounded her and excitedly told her all about the day's events.

"Wait till you see our goose," said her little brother. "'Tis a wonderful one!"

Mrs. Cratchit grabbed a platter from the

table and handed it to Peter, her oldest son. "Off with you to the baker's and collect the bird," she instructed him. "Take the children with you and no dallying."

Peter gladly took on this important task and led his brothers and sisters out the door. Once they were outside, Mrs. Cratchit had a moment to greet her daughter.

"Why, bless your heart alive, my dear," she said as she kissed Martha on the cheek. "How late you are."

"We had a deal of work to finish up last night," the young woman explained. "And had to clear away this morning."

Mrs. Cratchit helped Martha off with her shawl. "Never mind, so long as you're here," she said happily. "Sit down before the fire, Lord bless you."

"No, no," Belinda said excitedly as she looked out the window. "Father's coming. Hide, Martha."

Martha giggled as she quickly snuck into the closet and closed the door behind her.

Watching from above, Scrooge rolled his eyes at all the silliness. But the ghost smacked him in the head with the handle of his torch.

"Ow," Scrooge yelped. He turned to complain, but something about the ghost's appearance caught his eye. He noticed that small wrinkles had begun to form around the spirit's mouth and eyes. And his brown hair now had gray streaks at the temples. The ghost was aging right before his eyes.

The door burst open and when Scrooge looked down, he saw Bob Cratchit enter the house carrying his youngest son, Tiny Tim, on his shoulders.

Tiny Tim was small, even for a six-year-old. He carried a wooden crutch and wore iron braces on his legs. Once inside, Cratchit lifted Tim off his shoulders and handed him to Belinda, who helped him with his comforter. Tiny Tim was sickly, but his attitude and personality were the brightest in the family.

"Where's our Martha?" Cratchit asked.

Mrs. Cratchit shook her head sadly. "Not coming," she said.

"Not coming," Cratchit said, his happy mood suddenly deflated. "Not coming upon Christmas Day?"

Just then, the closet door burst open and Martha rushed across the room to her father.

"Here I am," she said as she wrapped him in a tight, warm hug.

"I'm so happy to see you." Cratchit beamed.

Belinda knew that Tim would love to see the washhouse where the desserts were cooling. "Come on, Timmy," she said. "Shall we have a look?"

"And how did little Tim behave," his mother asked once he had exited the room.

"Good as gold," Cratchit said as she handed him a stack of mismatched plates. "Somehow he gets thoughtful sitting by himself so much and thinks the strangest things you ever heard," he continued as he began arranging the plates on the table. "He told me while coming home that he hoped the people saw him in church, because he is a cripple and it might be pleasant to them to remember upon Christmas Day who made lame beggars walk and blind men see."

Both Mrs. Cratchit and Martha began to tear up at the story.

"I believe he grows stronger and more hearty every day my dear," Cratchit continued.

He turned to his wife and daughter, but neither said a word. They just nodded and smiled weakly, wiping away the tears when they heard Tim and Belinda walking into the room.

"The whole washhouse smells like a pastry shop," Tim announced.

Even the ghost was beginning to get choked with emotion. He sprinkled a small dose of dust over Cratchit and Tiny Tim. When he turned to look at Scrooge he saw something unusual. Scrooge had a look of actual compassion and concern as he looked down on the clerk and his family.

"Spirit, tell me," Scrooge said. "Will Tiny Tim . . ."

The spirit didn't even wait for Scrooge to finish the question. "I see a vacant seat in the poor chimney corner," he said, looking into the future. "And a crutch without an owner . . . carefully preserved."

Scrooge was overcome with sadness at the thought that Tiny Tim might not live much longer.

Suddenly, there was a loud roar below, and the rest of the Cratchit children paraded into the room carrying the roast goose. Peter ceremoniously placed the platter in the center of the table as everybody hustled to their seats.

Cratchit lifted Tiny Tim and sat him on a chair next to his own and then leaned over the steaming goose to inhale its delicious aroma.

"I don't believe I have ever seen a more magnificent goose," he said.

"'Tis a beautiful bird, that's for sure," Mrs. Cratchit said with a hint of disappointment in her voice. "But I pray that one Christmas the children might taste a turkey."

Cratchit nodded. He too wished that he could provide finer things for his family. "Perhaps one day," he said with a warm smile. Then he lifted his cup and everybody did likewise. "A toast, to Mr. Scrooge, the founder of our feast!"

Scrooge could not believe that he was being mentioned at the dinner. Neither could Mrs. Cratchit.

"The founder of our toast, indeed," she snarled as she jumped to her feet. "I wish I had him here. I'd give him a piece of my mind to feast upon. And, I hope he'd have a good appetite for it."

Scrooge withered and tried to hide behind

the ghost. But the spirit made sure Ebenezer could see it all.

"My dear," Cratchit protested to his wife. "The children. Christmas Day."

"Christmas Day, I am sure," she responded. "How can one drink the health of such an odious, stingy, hard, unfeeling man as Mr. Scrooge? You know he is, Robert. Nobody knows better than you."

Cratchit looked calmly at his wife and replied. "My dear. Christmas Day."

Mrs. Cratchit took a deep breath and looked at her husband for a moment before responding. "I'll drink his health for your sake and the day's, not for his."

Cratchit nodded in agreement, and she lifted her cup.

"A merry Christmas and a happy New Year," Mrs. Cratchit toasted. "He'll be very merry and happy, I have no doubt."

The other Cratchits raised their cups

halfheartedly to complete the toast.

Mrs. Cratchit regained her composure and once again raised her cup, this time much more happily as she toasted the entire family.

"A merry Christmas to us all, my dears," she called out. "God bless us!"

"God bless us!" they responded.

"God bless us, everyone!" Tiny Tim added.

Cratchit reached down and took hold of his son's little hand and clutched it tightly with a combination of love and pride.

Up above, Scrooge brushed a small tear from his cheek.

"Kind spirit," Scrooge pleaded, "say Tiny Tim will be spared."

The Ghost of Christmas Present shook his head sadly. "If these shadows remain unaltered by the future," he told Scrooge. "The child will die."

Ebenezer squeezed his eyes shut in sadness. "Die? No, spirit, no!"

"'If he is to die, he had better do it'"—as the ghost responded, his face turned into the spitting image of Scrooge himself—"'and decrease the surplus population.'"

Scrooge recognized what he had said earlier in the day to the two men who had come looking for charitable donations. He was ashamed to hear his words come back at him. Especially considering the condition of the little boy below.

The spirit's face returned to its normal shape, and Scrooge was struck speechless by embarrassment.

As the Cratchits said grace, the ghost sent the room racing out of London and across the countryside so fast that Scrooge was knocked down. Pressed against the clear floor and terrified that they might crash at any moment, Scrooge watched as the land sped beneath him at incredible speed.

Finally, the ghost brought the room to

a stop in a barren area surrounded by huge rock formations. It was cold and desolate.

"What place is this?" asked Scrooge.

"A place where miners live," said the spirit. "They labor in the bowels of the earth, yet they know me."

Scrooge looked down and saw a light shining through the window of a small hut. Scrooge and the spirit were lowered down into the hut until they could see a miner and his family sitting around a glowing fire. They were poor and humble, but their hearts were filled with Christmas joy as they sang "The First Noel."

"They know me," the spirit said, smiling warmly. "And have known my brothers for generations."

Before Scrooge could even respond, the ghost sent their chamber speeding across the countryside once again.

"Hold on," he warned as they took a violent turn. "It's going to be a bit bumpy!"

The Ghost of Christmas Present cackled as their flying chamber headed for the coast of England and raced over the roiling night sea. Scrooge was terrified as lightning and thunder crackled and boomed beneath them. The spirit zipped them in and out of the massive waves hurtling Scrooge from one side of the room to the other.

"I can't see a thing," Scrooge wailed, terrified of where they might be headed.

Suddenly, they spied a lone light cutting through the darkness ahead of them.

"Always go toward the light, Ebenezer," the ghost intoned. "Toward the light."

The light came and went. As they got closer, Scrooge realized that it was the beam from a lonely lighthouse built out on a sunken reef where huge waves came crashing down.

Inside the lighthouse, they could see two hardy lighthouse keepers, gray-haired men whose life was spent in quiet solitude away from the world. Still, they had the spirit of Christmas as they drank steaming cups of grog and sang.

A bolt of lightning struck right before Scrooge and the spirit, and when it did, they disappeared into a blinding light only to emerge on a different part of the ocean where things were calm.

"Listen," whispered the ghost as their room sailed just above the water's surface and approached a solitary ship at sea. The deck was lit by hundreds of lanterns and candles, and the crew were all topside celebrating the holiday and singing carols.

Each stop along the way made Scrooge more ashamed of his attitude. Finally, the room started climbing higher and higher into the night sky. As it did, the ghost sprinkled his magic dust, and the room started to spin. It spun slowly at first but picked up speed until the walls became a blur of color and light. Finally, there was a blinding flash and Scrooge closed his eyes and braced himself, thinking they were going to crash into the sea.

But they were no longer by the ocean. They were back in London, and when Scrooge dared to open his eyes, he was relieved to see that they were looking down into the parlor of a house. It was smartly decorated for the season, and in its center was a Christmas tree with handmade ornaments and glowing candles.

Scrooge smiled when he realized that this house belonged to his nephew, Fred, who was there with his wife and some family friends. They were all laughing and having a grand time.

Scrooge was not only relieved that they were away from the ocean but that the scene beneath him was pleasant. There were no sickly children or impoverished people to fill his heart with guilt. Maybe the painful part of his lesson was over.

The people were all playing a parlor game called Yes and No in which one person thinks of something and the others try to guess what it is by asking questions that can be answered with either a yes or a no.

"You're thinking of an animal," one of Fred's friends guessed.

"Yes," Fred answered with a smile.

"A live animal," guessed his sister-in-law.

"Yes," Fred said.

Scrooge could not help but get swept up into the game. Like the guests, he, too, tried to figure out what animal Fred had selected.

"A rather disagreeable animal," guessed Fred's wife.

"Yes!"

"An animal that growls and grunts?"

"And lives in London?"

Fred nodded and answered yes to both of them.

The guests all tried to think of what growling, disagreeable animals lived in London.

"A horse? A cow? A pig?"

With each of these guesses, Fred laughed and said no.

"A dog?" his wife guessed.

Now Fred really started to laugh.

"Yes and no," Fred answered.

Everyone was confused for a moment until his wife figured it out.

"I know what it is," she said with a laugh, and everyone turned to her, including Scrooge, who couldn't figure it out.

"What is it?"

"It's your Uncle Scrooge," she sang, and they all roared with laughter.

"Yes!" he said.

They had obviously talked about Fred's visit to the countinghouse and all the horrible things that Scrooge had said.

"'Christmas is a humbug,'" said one of Fred's friends. "He actually said that?"

Fred nodded. "And he believes it!"

Fred's wife was still laughing. "More shame on him."

Scrooge tried to look away, but the ghost

would not let him retreat and forced him to keep watching them.

"He's a comical old fellow, that's for sure," Fred continued. "Though not very pleasant."

"But very rich," his wife added.

"What of that, my dear?" Fred asked her. "His wealth is of no use to him. He does no good with it. Doesn't make himself comfortable with it. Is never going to benefit us with it."

His wife just shook her head. "I have no patience with him."

"I have," Fred said. "I'm sorry for him. Who suffers from his ill whims? Only himself. Here he decides to dislike us and won't come and dine with us. What's the consequence? He loses a dinner."

"Indeed, he loses a *very good* dinner," Fred's wife said proudly.

One of the guests raised his glass for a toast. "Here, here," he said. "A *magnificent* dinner."

The room filled with laughter as everyone

else raised their glasses and toasted along.

Although enjoying himself, Fred could not help but think of his sad uncle. "He has certainly given us plenty of merriment, that's for sure," he said. "And it would be ungrateful not to drink to his health. He wouldn't take it from me, but he may have it nevertheless. A merry Christmas to the old man, whatever he is. To Uncle Scrooge!"

He raised his cup again and everyone did likewise.

"To Uncle Scrooge."

Scrooge did not know what to make of the scenes that had played out beneath him. As much as they hurt, he knew they were right to speak of him that way. Yet, Cratchit still toasted him, and his nephew still wished him good cheer. Scrooge's beloved sister, Fan, had passed her good heart on to Fred.

Suddenly, the parlor beneath them started to transform, and their flying room broke free and headed off to their final destination. Scrooge was terrified of what might come next.

They reappeared inside a dark and eerie clock tower. There was no sign of their flying room. Instead, they were among thc churning gears and counterweights that ran the massive timepiece. Moonlight shone through the clock's face so that even though they were behind it, Scrooge could see that it was one minute to midnight.

He noticed that the ghost's torch had now burned out and that his face had grown very old. His once curly brown hair was now white as snow.

"Are spirit's lives so short?" Scrooge asked him.

The Ghost of Christmas Present looked at Ebenezer. "My life upon this globe is very brief," he said in a creaking voice. "It ends tonight."

"Tonight?"

"Tonight at midnight," he continued. "Hark! The time is drawing near."

They were interrupted by a loud clacking sound as the clock's machinery sputtered to life, about to signal midnight.

Scrooge looked back at the ghost and noticed a scrawny, skeletal talon poking out from the bottom of the spirit's robe.

"Forgive me, but I see something strange protruding from your skirt," he said. "Is it a foot or a claw?"

"It might be a claw," the spirit said. "For the scant amount of flesh there is upon it. Look here."

The spirit whipped open his robe to reveal two ragged, dirty children—a boy and a girl—angrily scowling and clutching onto the ghost's ankles.

Scrooge jumped back.

"Look here," the spirit wailed. "Look down here."

"Spirit?" Scrooge asked. "Are they yours?"

"They are man's," replied the ghost. "This

boy is *Ignorance*. This girl is *Want*. Beware of them both."

They grasped deeper into his ankle, and the spirit let loose a cry of anguish and pain.

"Have they no refuge?" Scrooge asked, pleading. "No resource?"

The massive clock began to chime the change in hour. Midnight had arrived, and the spirit began gasping. His day on Earth was almost over.

Suddenly, the boy transformed into a phantom reflection of his adult self. He was angry and menacing, a sinister thug who brandished a butcher knife.

"'Are there no prisons?'" the phantom said, mirroring the words Scrooge spoke to the men who'd come to his countinghouse seeking donations.

Next, the girl transformed into a specter of her future self. She was ugly and cackling, her tragic face caked with grotesque makeup.

"'Are there no workhouses?'" she said, echoing Scrooge's other retort to the men.

That's when Scrooge realized they represented *his* Ignorance, *his* Want. These demons were projections of his own dark and sinister heart.

Scrooge reeled back in terror as the hammer continued to strike the bells inside the clock. Finally, the hammer struck for a twelfth and final time. Midnight had arrived, and the once mighty Ghost of Christmas Present gasped his final breath. He died before Scrooge, and his body dissolved first into a corpse, then into a skeleton, and finally into sparkling dust. The tremor of the final bell toll rattled the floor and scattered the dust.

Scrooge was now all alone in the clockworks.

Ebenezer tried to catch his breath, but he noticed something that caused him to panic. The moonlight cast a long shadow of him, and before his eyes that shadow began to come alive and separate into two.

One of the shadows continued to grow and grow, its massive form perfectly silhouetted by the full moon. Scrooge trembled as he looked upon this phantom shadow, for he knew what it was and he knew it was the one thing he feared most.

Chapter 5

The inner workings of the clock had quieted, and Scrooge trembled with fear as he stared at the phantom specter growing larger in front of his eyes. This spirit had no face or features of any kind. It was just a dark shadow that loomed above him ominously.

Scrooge dropped to his knees and clasped his hands together. "Am I in the presence of the Ghost of Christmas Yet to Come?" he asked, his teeth chattering.

The specter did not move or respond in any way. Despite the silence, Scrooge knew exactly what stood before him.

"You are about to show me shadows of the things that have not yet happened but will happen," Scrooge exclaimed. "Is that so, spirit?"

Scrooge shook uncontrollably, but the ghost remained perfectly silent and still.

"Ghost of the future," he said, near tears, "I fear you more than any specter I have seen! But I know your purpose is to do me good. I am prepared to bear you company. Lead me."

The spirit still refused to move or respond in the slightest, and this silence shook Scrooge to the core. This was the visit he had been dreading the most, and he wanted to get it over with.

"The night is waning fast," Scrooge told the specter. "It's precious time to me. Lead on, spirit."

The anger in Scrooge's voice enraged the spirit. Suddenly it tore its silhouette away from the surface of the mist and lunged directly at Scrooge.

Terrified, Scrooge fell backward, but rather than hit the floor, he continued to fall, tumbling head over heels down a long and narrow spiral staircase.

It was an agonizing fall, and Scrooge slammed his head and tailbone into step after step before mercifully coming to a stop at the stairway's bottom.

When he caught his breath and sat up, he found himself outside the entrance to the Royal Exchange. This relieved him greatly. Scrooge was proud to be a member of the exchange and when he looked up he saw three men who he recognized, although he could not quite remember their names. They had no awareness of him or of the fact that he had just passed right through their bodies when he landed.

"When did he die?" asked one.

"Last night I believe," another answered. "Or sometime on Christmas Day."

The third man just shook his head. "I

thought he'd never die. What was the matter with him?"

"God knows," the first said with a yawn.

The second man raised an eyebrow as he asked, "What's he done with his money?"

"He hasn't left it to me," one answered with a shrug. "That's all I know."

This was greeted by a laugh, and Scrooge could not help but wonder why the spirit wanted him to hear such trivial conversation. They weren't even interested in the dead man, why should he be?

"It's likely to be a cheap funeral," the third one said. "I don't know anyone who'd go to it."

"I don't mind going," one said with a laugh. "If a lunch is provided."

Still dazed by his fall, Scrooge staggered up to his feet. Maybe he was supposed to wander outside the exchange and find a conversation that would help him with his lesson. But when he got up to do so, all of the people who had lined the street disappeared. Suddenly, Ebenezer Scrooge was all alone on Threadneedle Street. Snow fell silently, and Scrooge looked for any signs of life.

All he saw was the spirit's shadow slithering over the stairs of the exchange. When he turned to see the phantom itself, there were only the flickering gaslights that lined the street.

This spirit was nothing more than a shadow. Scrooge looked at it, and the finger of the shadow pointed down the street. Ebenezer followed its path and saw a horse-drawn hearse appear at the end of the street.

Scrooge wondered if perhaps it had something to do with the dead man the three were just talking about. Then he recognized it. It was the hearse that had pulled Jacob Marley to his grave seven years ago. It was the same ghostly hearse that had chased Scrooge up the stairs of his house earlier that Christmas Eve.

When the horses turned toward Scrooge,

steam rose off their warm bodies and from their flaring nostrils.

Scrooge gulped and slowly backed away. The shadowy finger turned and pointed right at him.

With a crack of the whip from the driver, the horses started pulling the hearse down the street, charging straight for Scrooge.

Ebenezer tried to scurry out of the way, but his slippers had no traction and no matter how fast he pumped his legs, they flailed uselessly.

The horses increased their gallop and continued right toward him, the driver carefully righting the hearse as its wheels slid side to side along the icy road.

Scrooge's slippers finally gained a shred of traction, and he started running wildly away from the oncoming hearse.

It was too late.

As the vehicle reached him, the driver stood for a final crack of the whip. But this one was aimed at Scrooge himself. It cracked just above his head with a thunderous roar that literally shook him to the bone. The shock wave echoed throughout the street, and in its wake buildings melted and cobblestones shattered. The entire world seemed to collapse upon the terrified old man.

Scrooge held his head in agony and crumpled to the ground. As he did, Threadneedle Street ceased to exist and the setting changed into a dark and dirty alleyway.

In the alleyway, everything seemed to be growing. Buildings stretched out of proportion. People stretched into gigantic shapes. Then Scrooge realized that they weren't growing—he was shrinking. He was getting smaller by the second, but he had no time to consider this because the hearse continued to chase him.

He looked back over his shoulder and saw that the spirit was now driving the hearse. And as the stallions' hooves slammed the cobblestones around him, Scrooge saw the phantom leap from the hearse and straddle the backs of the horses.

By this time, Scrooge was no bigger than a rat, and the spirit reached its shadowy arm down to the ground and grabbed him, surrounding him in darkness.

After a long moment, the darkness gave way to the tiniest bit of light and Scrooge was once again his normal size. He found himself in a cold and dreary room, devoid of almost all color. In the middle of the room was a bed. A shaft of unearthly pale light outlined a human form covered by an old, ragged sheet. It was, Scrooge knew instantly, the dead man of whom the others had spoken so contemptuously.

A candle flickered on the nightstand by the bed and cast a shadow of the phantom on the wall. The spirit pointed its finger at the body, for Scrooge to look.

"This is a fearful place," he told the spirit. "When I leave it, I shall not leave its lesson. Trust me. Let's go."

Once again, the phantom pointed toward the body.

"I understand, and I would if I could," Scrooge said, terrified to look at the face of the corpse. "But I have not the power."

The ghost turned so that its unseen eyes were focused right on Scrooge.

Ebenezer could not bear the sight of this dead body left all alone, with no one to mourn or miss him. He was almost certain that the body was his.

"If there is any person who feels emotion caused by this man's death," he pleaded, "show that person to me. I beg you."

Suddenly, a burst of light enveloped them, and when it passed, Scrooge and the phantom were inside a modest home. Scrooge did not recognize the house or the young mother rocking a baby in her arms. A door opened and her husband walked in.

This man also seemed completely unfamiliar, and Scrooge could not figure out how this family might feel emotion at the death of the man he feared was himself.

"Is it good or bad?" the woman asked.

"Bad," the man said, biting his lip.

The woman looked down at the floor. "Are we ruined?"

"No," her husband answered. "There is hope yet."

She shook her head. "Only if he relents."

"He's past relenting," said the man, now beginning to smile. "He's dead."

"Thank God," the woman shouted with glee. Moments later she felt guilty for greeting the news this way and asked a silent prayer of forgiveness.

"To whom will our debts be transferred?" she continued.

"I don't know. But then we'll be ready with the money," he assured her. "And even if we're not, it's unlikely any new creditor could ever be so merciless. We can sleep tonight with light hearts."

Scrooge was devastated. When he asked to see emotion tied to the death, he did not imagine that emotion would be happiness. Before he could say a word, the images faded away and Ebenezer once again found himself in the room with the dead man.

The phantom pointed and again Scrooge pleaded with him.

"Let me see some tenderness connected with a death," he begged the spirit. "Or this dark chamber will forever haunt me."

Another light enveloped them, and this time they were transported to the Cratchit house. Scrooge found himself standing on the narrow staircase, and the fire from the fireplace cast the phantom's shadow on the wall beside him.

Ebenezer looked down at the family table, the same one at which he'd seen the joyous Christmas dinner. But now it was solemn. Mrs. Cratchit sat with her children. The mood in the room was very different from before. The happiness of the holiday had been replaced with quiet and sadness.

"And He took a child and set him in the midst of them," the eldest son, Peter, read from the Bible. Once he was done, he closed the book and set it on the table in front of him.

"It's late," Mrs. Cratchit said, looking at the clock. "It's past your father's time."

Her son looked up at her. "He's walked slower these last few evenings."

"He has walked with Tiny Tim on his shoulder fast indeed," Mrs. Cratchit said, her voice cracking with sadness. "But he was very light to carry, and your father loved him so."

A moment later, Bob Cratchit came in through the door. The children got up to greet him and though he gave them hugs, there was a definite sadness about him. His boyish charm and enthusiasm were gone. He seemed much older than before. He had just come back from the cemetery.

Mrs. Cratchit looked at her husband and tried to smile. "You went today?"

"Yes, my dear," Cratchit said as he sat by the fire. "I wish you could have gone. It would have done you good to see how green a place it is. But you'll see it often. I promised him that I would walk there every Sunday."

It was at this point that Bob Cratchit began to cry. "Oh, my child," he wailed. "My little child."

The children surrounded him and did their best to console him. It was a gesture he greatly appreciated.

"I am sure none of us shall ever forget our poor Tiny Tim," he said.

"Never, Father," the children replied.

"Thank you, my dears," he told them. Cratchit hugged each of his children and climbed up the narrow staircase. At one point it seemed as though he and Scrooge were looking each other in the eye, but the clerk had no true awareness of the spirit that was watching him.

Tears filled Scrooge's eyes as he watched Cratchit enter a small room. In the middle of the room was a bed and on that bed lie the dead body of Tiny Tim. This room was the opposite of the one with the other corpse. It was brightly lit and fully decorated for Christmas. It was the room of a person who had been truly loved in life.

Cratchit bent over and kissed Tim's forehead, and then he sat next to the bed and began to sob.

Scrooge was overcome with grief and fear. He turned to the spirit. "Specter, something tells me our parting moment is at hand," he said. "Tell me. Who was that man we saw lying dead?"

The spirit waved his shadow of an arm, and a tornado-force wind whipped through the house, tearing it into a thousand pieces. When the wind had passed, Scrooge found himself alone in a dark and desolate churchyard.

Scrooge slowly walked across the frozen ground of the cemetery as gnarled trees swayed in the winter wind. A full moon cast its light across the graveyard, and with it came the terrifying shadow of the Ghost of Christmas Yet to Come. It pointed to a lonely, untended gravestone, away from the others and overrun by weeds.

Scrooge knew that he must proceed and read the name on the stone, but before he could, he turned and pleaded once more with the haunting spirit.

"Before I draw nearer to that stone to which you point," Scrooge said. "Answer me one question. Are these the shadows of things that *will* be. Or shadows of things that *may* be?"

Again the ghost gestured to the headstone

as the wind caused ripples to pass through his indistinct form.

"Men's courses in life foreshadow certain ends," Scrooge continued. "But if these courses are departed from, these ends will change. Isn't that so?"

The shadow lowered its arm and revealed the name on the marker. It read: EBENEZER SCROOGE.

Scrooge dropped to his knees and cried out. "Am I the man who lay upon the bed?"

The phantom unleashed a gust of wind that blew away some of the snow covering the bottom of the headstone. It read: BORN FEBRUARY 7, 1786.

Suddenly, another gust came and slowly pushed away the snow that covered Scrooge's date of death.

"Hear me!" Scrooge shouted, terrified of learning the day he would die. "I'm not the man I was. Why show me this if I'm past all hope?"

The snow blew away and uncovered more of

the date, showing that he would die on December twenty-fifth—Christmas Day.

"Good spirit, assure me that I may change these shadows you have shown me," he cried as the snow began to uncover the year of his death.

As he begged, his feet slowly began to sink into the ground above his grave. He tried to climb out, but that only opened the ground even more. Suddenly, all of the dirt fell out from beneath him and Scrooge was at the top of a giant hole. He grabbed on to a protruding tree branch and dangled above the grave.

Ebenezer looked down into the hole and to his horror saw a coffin resting beneath him. He let out a bloodcurdling scream as the lid of the coffin opened, revealing the box to be empty.

"Help, spirit!" he screamed as the branch began to break free, lowering him closer and closer to the pine box below.

He looked up and saw that the phantom was

now staring down at him. And for the first time, he saw something other than shadow. He saw two glowing eyes filled with death and terror. They pierced right through him.

"No, spirit," he pleaded. "I will honor Christmas in my heart and try to keep it all the year."

The phantom's eyes flared.

"I will not shut out the lessons of the past, nor the present, nor the future!" Scrooge yelled. "Tell me I may sponge away the writing on that stone!"

The phantom reached down to him and Scrooge did not know what to do. There was no way to grab hold of a shadow. There was no way this spirit could help him. But as the phantom's eyes narrowed, Scrooge suddenly felt a sense of peacefulness.

He let go of the branch and fell down into the grave, his arms and legs flailing. He spun over and fell facedown, heading straight for the coffin. Right before he hit, he closed his eyes and braced for impact.

But it never came.

He was stopped cold by some unseen force and left dangling. Scrooge carefully opened his eyes, and just a hair's breadth before him he saw a bull's-eye–shaped knot in the wood.

Chapter 6

Although he did not yet realize it, Scrooge was not dangling above his coffin. He was upside down in his bedchamber. His legs were somehow tangled in the curtains that surrounded his bed. His pointy nose hovered just an inch above the bull's-eye knothole in a floorboard.

It took a moment for him to realize that he was in fact not dead and that he was actually in his bedchamber and not his coffin.

When the picture fully crystallized and he knew that he had survived the visit from Marley's three spirits, Ebenezer let out a gleeful cheer like none he had ever yelled before.

"Yee-ha!"

Just then the curtains snapped, and Scrooge slammed into the floor nose first. It did not matter one whit. He bounced right up on his feet, tears streaming down his cheeks and a giant smile on his face.

"They're still here," he shouted as he clutched the now-torn bed curtains. "*I'm* still here!"

He began exhibiting some very un-Scrooge-like behavior as he hopped, skipped, and danced his way around the room.

"I don't know what to do!" he exclaimed. "I'm light as a feather, merry as a schoolboy. I'm as giddy as a drunken man."

He hurried over to the window and flung it open. The previous day's gloom had given way to a bright blue sky. There was no longer any fog or mist, just golden sunlight. Ebenezer took a deep breath of the cold, fresh air and was invigorated. Down below he saw a boy pulling his red sleigh through the snow. It was the same boy he had seen with the Ghost of Christmas Present. Only now, unlike before, he could interact with the young man.

"What's today, fine fellow?" he called out.

The boy stopped and looked up. "Today?" he said as if of all days this should be the most obvious. "Why, Christmas Day!"

"Christmas Day," Scrooge sang like a song to himself. "I haven't missed it. The spirits have done it all in one night. They can do anything they like."

"My fine fellow," he called back down to the boy. "Do you know the poulterer's on the corner?"

The boy nodded. "I should hope I do."

"What an intelligent boy," Scrooge responded. "Do you know whether they've sold the prize turkey that was hanging there? Not the little prize turkey . . . the big one?"

"The one as big as me?"

Scrooge laughed. "Yes!"

The boy nodded. "It's hanging there now."

"It is?" Scrooge said as he concocted his plan. "Go and buy it!"

The boy looked at Scrooge, trying to figure out if this was all some sort of trick.

"I am in earnest," the old man replied. "Buy it and bring it here, and I'll give you a shilling. Come back in less than five minutes and I'll give you a half-crown."

A half-crown was a lot of money to the boy, and he was off like a shot to the store.

Scrooge smiled as the boy hurried down the street. "I'll send it to Bob Cratchit's," he said aloud to himself with a belly laugh. "He shan't know who sent it. It's twice the size of Tiny Tim."

Scrooge hurried down the stairs into the foyer of his house, when he suddenly saw something that stopped him in his tracks.

"Mrs. Dilber," he cried, throwing his arms wide open.

Mrs. Dilber, the cleaning lady, had just

entered, spun, and jumped back against the door. Her jaw dropped at the sight of her boss still in his nightgown and grinning like a fool. Terrified, she started to unlock the door to run.

"Merry Christmas!" Scrooge announced as he took her by the arms and started dancing across the entryway. "My dear Mrs. Dilber, you're the loveliest creature I have ever laid eyes upon. Dance with me!"

"Eeeeee!" Mrs. Dilber screamed as she broke free of Scrooge's grip and rushed to the back of the house screaming hysterically.

"What a charming woman," he said with a chuckle, totally unaffected by her sense of panic.

A few minutes later, Scrooge had gotten dressed and was about to leave his house. At the door, he stopped and turned to face the knocker, the one that had terrified him when it turned into Marley's face the night before.

"I shall love it as long as I live," he said, giving the knocker a kiss. "What an honest face it has."

Just then, the boy from the street came back to Scrooge's house. "Here's the bird!"

The boy motioned to the burly poulterer trudging up the path. Although he was strong, the man was straining to carry the massive turkey fully cooked and dressed—ready for Christmas dinner.

"Merry Christmas," Scrooge said happily as he greeted the poulterer. He let out a whistle of admiration as he looked at the massive turkey. "Why, it's impossible to carry that to Camden Town. You must have a cab."

Scrooge turned and signaled for a horse-drawn hackney cab. When it pulled up, Scrooge helped the poulterer get into the cab with the giant bird and gave the driver directions to Bob Cratchit's house.

He smiled broadly as he watched the cab pull

away. He imagined how happy the Cratchits would be when the turkey was delivered, and it was almost more excitement than he could stand. He was so happy that when a carriage rode by he instantly thought back to the boys he had once called delinquents for hanging on to the back of a carriage and letting it pull them across the icy street. Now he wanted to try it himself.

He grabbed hold and let out a merry *wheeee* as he skied along the street, drawing stares of amazement from nearly everyone who saw him.

For the first time, Scrooge loved walking among the people filling the streets with Christmas cheer. When he had ridden above the landscape with the Ghost of Christmas Present, he had been so distant from the feelings of happiness and joy. Now, though, he was part of everything, and it was exhilarating.

"Good morning to you," he said to strangers walking past him. "Merry Christmas!" Then a familiar face caught his attention. It was the large man who had come to Scrooge's countinghouse looking for donations for the poor. Ebenezer strode right up to him and took him by the shoulders.

"My dear sir, how do you do?" Scrooge said as if he were greeting a long-lost friend. "I hope you succeeded yesterday. A merry Christmas to you."

"Mr. Scrooge?" the man said warily.

"Yes, that is my name," Scrooge said, nodding. "And I fear it may not be pleasant to you. But allow me to ask your pardon. And will you have the goodness . . ."

Scrooge leaned forward and whispered the promise of a huge donation into the man's ear.

"Lord bless me!" the man said, overwhelmed by the amount. "My dear Mr. Scrooge, are you serious?"

"And not a farthing less," Scrooge said with a definitive nod of the head. "A great many back payments are included in it, I assure you."

The man was so moved by emotion that he was momentarily speechless. "My dear sir, I don't know what to say. . . ."

Scrooge cut him off and gave him a reassuring pat on the back. "Don't say anything," he told the man. "I am much obliged to you. Many thanks to you, and God bless you."

Scrooge tipped his hat, smiled, and continued down High Street. The man watched him go in stunned amazement, unable to believe that this Scrooge was the same man who had treated him and his cause so rudely just the day before.

But it wasn't. Certainly, the body of Scrooge was the same, but the spirit inside of that body had changed greatly. And that spirit was glowing with the joy of the holiday. For so long Scrooge had detested the songs of the carolers, but as he heard them now they filled his heart with happiness.

Ebenezer practically danced along the street

to the music of the carolers and the sounds of the glorious church bells. He continued all the way until he reached the warm and happy home that belonged to his nephew Fred. As he approached the door, Scrooge could hear the muffled laughter of the party inside.

For a moment, his happiness faded away. He could not bring himself to knock on the door. He was too sad and ashamed of the way he had behaved for so many years. He was embarrassed at the treatment that he had shown the son of his beloved sister, Fan. He turned to go home, but then a particularly loud boom of laughter stopped him in his tracks.

Just maybe the spirit of Christmas was enough for him to be forgiven. He took a deep breath, reached up and rapped on the door with a bony hand. A moment later the door opened, and Scrooge saw the smiling face of a housemaid.

"Is your master home?" he asked pleasantly.

"Yes, sir," the woman said, trying to recognize Scrooge's face, which of course she couldn't because he had never once taken the time to visit his nephew.

"I am his uncle," he said.

The woman let him in, and Scrooge walked slowly to the parlor where Fred and his friends were playing. He had watched the game alongside the Ghost of Christmas Present and knew that he had been ridiculed, but now he hoped that he could also be welcomed.

They were playing the game Yes and No.

"An animal that growls and grunts?" one of the guests asked.

"Yes," Fred replied.

"And lives in London?" another questioned.

"Yes!" he answered.

For a moment Scrooge waited outside the doorway, pained with the knowledge of how they saw him. He listened as they guessed all sorts of animals. A cow and a pig. Fred said no to each until his wife guessed dog.

Fred smiled and answered, "Yes and no!"

This brought a laugh from everyone. They were all laughing so hard and enjoying themselves so much that none of them noticed that Scrooge had entered the parlor.

The scene was almost exactly as it had been the night before when he watched it with the spirit.

"I know what it is, Fred," offered his sister-in-law.

"What is it?" Fred asked.

"It's your . . ." But before she could finish her statement, Fred completed it on his own.

"Uncle Scrooge!" Only he wasn't trying to answer the question, he was looking at his uncle directly across the room from him.

"Why, bless my soul," Fred continued, a look of total shock on his face.

They all turned to look at Ebenezer, and everyone was wearing the same expression.

To their amazement, Ebenezer Scrooge was standing in the parlor, wearing his best clothes.

"I have come to dinner," Scrooge said meekly. "If you'll have me."

Fred's wife happily jumped to her feet. "Have you?" she said as she gave him a warm embrace. "Mercy! Come in, please. Fred, introduce your uncle."

Fred rushed over and shook his uncle's hand so hard it throbbed with pain, but Scrooge didn't mind one bit.

Later that night, Scrooge sat down for a delicious dinner of Christmas goose, holiday treats, desserts, and punch. It was the happiest he could ever remember feeling.

Epilogue

It was the day after Christmas, and a gentle snow was falling on London. Scrooge sat at the desk in his countinghouse and looked out the window. He saw Bob Cratchit hurrying down the street.

"A full sixteen minutes late," Scrooge said gleefully as he checked the time on his pocket watch. Suddenly, he remembered the joke that the Cratchit daughters had pulled on their father, and he decided to do likewise. He replaced his happy expression with the familiar scowl he had worn for so long.

The door creaked open, and Cratchit slinked

over to his desk. He didn't even take the time to remove his hat or jacket before he furiously began working at his desk, hoping beyond hope that Scrooge had not noticed that he was late.

"What do you mean by coming here at this time of day?" Scrooge growled at him.

"I am very sorry, sir," Cratchit said nervously. "I am behind my time."

"You are, indeed," Scrooge replied. "Step in here."

Cratchit closed his eyes in worry, certain that his boss was going to fire him for being late. He stepped into Scrooge's office. "It's only once a year, sir," he said, trembling. "It shall not be repeated. I was making rather merry yesterday."

Scrooge fought the urge to smile and continued his act. He threw down his pen in mock anger. "Now, I'll tell you what, Mr. Cratchit," he said as he marched over to the clerk, "I am not going to stand for this sort of thing any longer."

Cratchit's face turned white, and he was about to faint.

"And therefore," Scrooge said, his scowl suddenly turning into a giant smile. "I'm about to raise your salary!"

Scrooge laughed gleefully, and Cratchit had no idea what to think. Ebenezer put a supportive hand on his clerk's shoulder and greeted him warmly. "A merry Christmas, Bob! A merrier Christmas my good fellow than I've given you in many years. I'll raise your salary and do whatever I can to help your struggling family. And we'll discuss your affairs this very afternoon over a bowl of Christmas punch! But first, let's make the fires."

Scrooge shoved a pouch of coins into Cratchit's hand. "I want you to go out and buy another scuttle of coal," he said with a wink. "Before you dot another *I*, Bob Cratchit."

Cratchit did not know what to do. His first reaction was that his boss had gone mad. But there was something about his voice that made Cratchit realize his words were heartfelt. Scrooge was a changed man.

"Off with you, Bob." Scrooge laughed. "We've got wassailing to do!"

Cratchit smiled at the thought of his boss dancing with Christmas joy. "Yes, sir," he said happily. "Right away."

Bob Cratchit staggered weakly out into the street from the countinghouse, still uncertain what to make of all this. He lifted his hat for a moment to scratch his head, unsure if he should buy the coal or perhaps go find a doctor to examine Mr. Scrooge.

He looked back through the window and saw the old man dancing a jolly jig and practicing his wassail. Scrooge laughed gleefully, and Bob Cratchit nodded with great warmth and happiness. There would be no need for a doctor and no need to worry about the darkness inside Scrooge's heart.

Like Bob Cratchit, many others would wonder what to make of the changed man that Ebenezer had become. Over the years, some would point and stare. But Scrooge never once let it get to him. It had been a great gift that Jacob Marley and the three spirits had given him. The gift of knowing the truth that beat inside him. The gift of a second chance in order to redeem himself.

There would be no need for Scrooge to trudge through the afterlife chained to his earthly possessions. He went on to be even better than his word to Cratchit. He did all he said he would and more.

From then on he greeted every day—especially Christmas Day—with the hopes of peace on Earth and goodwill to all.

To Tiny Tim, Scrooge became like a second father, helping him to grow strong and even carrying him when need be. The vision of the Ghost of Christmas Present did not come to pass. Tim grew healthier and healthier, spending many happy days with his family and with Ebenezer.

Scrooge went on to become as good a friend and master and as good a man as the good old city ever knew. He had no further involvement with the spirits, and it was always said of him that he knew how to keep Christmas well.

May that truly be said of us, and of all of us. And, as Tiny Tim observed, "God bless us, everyone!"